Little
Sparkles

Party at the Pool

Collect all the

LITTLE SPARKLES

1. Party in the Garden
2. Party at the Zoo
3. Party at the Pool
4. Party on the Pirate Ship
5. Party in the castle

Little Sparkles

Party at the Pool

Emily Moon

SCHOLASTIC

First published in the UK in 2012 by Scholastic Children's Books
An imprint of Scholastic Ltd
Euston House, 24 Eversholt Street
London, NW1 1DB, UK
Registered office: Westfield Road, Southam, Warwickshire, CV47 0RA
SCHOLASTIC and associated logos are trademarks and/or
registered trademarks of Scholastic Inc.
Series created by Working Partners Ltd.

ISBN 978 1407 12458 2

A CIP catalogue record for this book
is available from the British Library.

Printed and bound by CPI Group (UK) Ltd., Croydon, CR0 4YY
Papers used by Scholastic Children's Books
are made from wood grown in sustainable forests.

1 3 5 7 9 10 8 6 4 2

www.scholastic.co.uk/zone

With special thanks to Dawn McNiff

For Eddie and Ester, with love

Dear Holly & Rose,

Please come to my birthday party at the Aqua Adventure Pool!

It's on Saturday at 3 o'clock.

Bring your swimming costumes and make a splash!

Love,
Maisie

1

Watery Wonderland

"I hope there's a gigantic water slide to zoom down," cried Rose, running up the path to the Aqua Adventure Pool with Holly, her twin sister.

"And I can't wait to practise my front crawl," said Holly. She swung her flowery cloth bag, which was stuffed with a pink towel and a birthday present wrapped in crinkly paper. "Maisie's swimming party is going to be so much fun!"

The twins' long, toffee-coloured plaits bounced as they ran. They were wearing matching T-shirts with a picture of a seashell on the front, jeans and trainers. Underneath, they already had on their sparkly green swimming costumes. The only way to tell them apart was their waterproof watches – Holly's was green and Rose's was pink.

They stopped by the entrance. The pool was brand new and the big glass building gleamed in the sunshine. Clouds and swooping birds were reflected in the huge windows.

"Hey, Rose, do you think the Little Sparkles will come to Maisie's party today?" asked Holly.

"Oh, I hope so!" said Rose. "Especially if the Party Poopers turn up."

The twins shared a wonderful secret. They were friends with the Little Sparkles – tiny, magical creatures who protected parties from the Party Poopers. The naughty Poopers spoiled party games, turned the food bad and even hid

birthday presents. But the girls had discovered a way to stop them: by getting the Poopers to have fun! Whenever a Pooper enjoyed itself, it transformed into a brand new Little Sparkle.

"You two ran fast," called Mum, walking up the path towards them. The sunshine glinted on her sunglasses. "We're half an hour early, so let's wait outside until everyone arrives."

Holly and Rose peered inside the glass building. They could see a giant oval pool. No one was swimming in it yet, and the water looked calm and perfectly blue. Beside it was a little shell-shaped pool for babies. Bubbling rapids gushed along a

narrow passageway, and at the back was a tall blue slide. It wound like a corkscrew from the ceiling right down into the water.

"The new pool's amazing," cried Holly.

Mum nodded. "And you and the other guests will have the whole place to yourselves," she said. "Aren't you lucky?"

An older girl appeared by the window. She had a whistle hanging from a cord around her neck and was mopping the tiled floor.

"It's Ella!" said Rose.

Mum nodded. "Yes, she's got a job as the Aqua Adventure Pool lifeguard."

Ella was their friend Billy's big sister, and sometimes looked after the twins when Mum and Dad were out.

"Hi, Ella!" called Holly. The twins knocked on the glass.

Ella stopped mopping and grinned when she saw Holly and Rose. She waved at them to come into the pool.

"Can we go in now, Mum?" asked Rose, jumping up and down. "Oh, please!"

"OK," said Mum, waving back at Ella. "I know Ella will look after you. But make sure you do what she says."

"We promise," chorused Holly and Rose.

They kissed Mum goodbye and raced to the pool entrance. But just before they got to the door, a wave of water splashed against the glass.

"What was that?" wondered Holly.

They stopped and stared inside once more. Another wave shot up from the shell-shaped baby pool, and there,

bobbing around in the shallow water, were three little grey blobs.

"Oh no – it's the Party Poopers!" cried Rose.

2

Magical Meddling

Inside the pool building, the twins skidded to a halt.

"We're here for Maisie's party," Holly explained to the woman sitting at the reception desk. "I'm Holly and this is Rose."

The woman pointed towards a door to the side. "The changing rooms are through there. Have fun!"

"Thank you!" the twins replied at once.

They went into a room filled with benches and lockers. Soon they were only wearing their swimming costumes and watches.

"Come on," said Holly, stuffing her T-shirt into the flowery bag. "We've got to get rid of the Poopers before they ruin Maisie's party."

The twins hurried to a row of lockers, moving carefully so that they wouldn't slip on the damp floor.

Rose grabbed the handle of one of the lockers and pulled. It wouldn't budge, so Holly held on too and they yanked it together.

WHOOSH! The locker door flew open in a burst of colourful glitter. Out floated

a tiny turtle with a rainbow-coloured shell, holding a little party bag. He was so small he could have sat in the girls' hands.

Holly and Rose gasped. It was Tubbs, one of the Little Sparkles.

"Oh, Tubbs," cried Rose. "How lovely

to see you! But what were you doing in the locker?"

"The Poopers shut me in there," Tubbs explained, a deep frown on his face. "And I don't know where the other Little Sparkles are."

"Don't worry," said Rose, shoving the girls' things into the locker. "We'll find them. Maybe the rest of the Little Sparkles are shut in here too."

"Bubbles!" Holly called. "Princess!"

"Tikki! Peppy!" added Rose. "Are you here?"

But there was no answer, so the twins and Tubbs pushed through a door into the pool area. Tubbs floated right past

Ella, who was stacking a heap of floats into a neat pile. The girls knew that Ella couldn't see him, anyway. Peppy the puppy had explained that the girls were special, because they were the only people who could see the Little Sparkles and Party Poopers. The twins hadn't told anyone else their secret.

"Hi, guys!" said Ella. But then she sighed. "Everything's in a right mess. Come and see."

She led the twins along the poolside to the eating area. The tables and chairs were decorated to look like a beach cove, with strings of pretty shells, plastic seaweed and palm trees, and a ship's anchor.

But lots of the seaweed was ripped. The anchor was bent, and the palm trees' leaves were hanging off.

"How awful!" cried Rose.

"Even the party bags are ruined," said Ella, pointing to a table in the corner.

The fish-shaped bags were crumpled and the sweets that should have been inside them were scattered everywhere. Jelly octopuses and chocolate pebbles lay in a jumble on the floor.

"I don't know how it happened," said Ella, shaking her head. "Everything was fine earlier."

As she knelt down to gather up some ripped seaweed, the twins exchanged

a knowing glance.

"I know just what's gone on here," whispered Rose. "It was the Poopers!"

Tubbs floated up to join the girls. "I can't find my friends anywhere," he said with a sniff, "and I'm the only Little Sparkle who can swim. What if they've fallen in the water?"

Rose glanced at her waterproof watch. "Maisie and everyone else will be here in twenty minutes," she said.

Holly felt her tummy twist into a knot of worry. "How will we find the Little Sparkles before then – and get rid of the Poopers?"

3

Look Out, Little Sparkles!

Rose put her hand on Holly's shoulder. "We can't give up," she said. "Come on, let's help Tubbs search."

Ella had wheeled over a trolley full of cleaning equipment and was wiping the tables and chairs. While her back was turned, the twins and Tubbs went to the other side of the pool to look for the Little Sparkles. A flash of movement by the refreshment stand caught Rose's eye. A

bottle of cola was rolling across the floor – being pushed by a hairy grey blobby creature.

"It's a Pooper!" she cried, nudging Holly.

The Pooper rolled the bottle right to the edge of the pool. Then he unscrewed the bottle top and let the dark, fizzing liquid pour into the water.

"Stop!" cried Rose.

But the Pooper just laughed, and chanted:

> *"Tip the bottles upside down,*
> *Turn the pool a mucky brown.*
> *Let Lazy-Maisie cry and frown,*
> *Her drippy party's the worst in*
> *town!"*

The twins and Tubbs rushed over to the Pooper, but they were too late. The clear blue water had turned brown and cloudy. With a snigger, the Pooper chucked the empty bottle into the pool and darted behind the refreshments stand.

"The Poopers are making the party worse and worse!" Rose groaned.

Tubbs nodded, but Rose could see that he was fidgeting with worry. He rubbed his front feet together and wagged his tiny tail.

"It's all right, Tubbs," said Holly. "We'll find your friends before we stop the Poopers. But where could they be?"

Holly glanced around the pool. "Tubbs, you could dive in and search the water. Rose and I can go up the tall slide and see if we can spot them from up there."

Tubbs saluted her, grinning, then swooped away in a swish of glitter. There

was a small splash as he dived into the pool.

Holly ran over to where Ella was fixing a palm tree and asked if they could use the slide.

"Of course you can," Ella said. "Just be careful."

The girls climbed up the long flight of steps that led up to the slide. They were panting for breath when they reached the top. Even though she was worried about the missing Little Sparkles, Rose couldn't help smiling as she gazed down at the pool. From over the top of the railing she could see the oval main pool and the passageway of wild rapids looping out from it. Bobbing near the entrance to the rapids was a small blow-up raft.

Rose gazed down at the raft. She realized that a stack of armbands at the side of the pool meant that the raft couldn't be seen from ground level.

Narrowing her eyes, she could just make out four tiny figures perched on it.

"There they are!" she cried.

Peppy the blue puppy was sitting next to Tikki the yellow kitten, with Bubbles the pink bunny and Princess the purple and white pony knelt behind them. They all seemed to be looking around.

"I think they're searching for the Poopers," said Holly.

But creeping along the edge of the pool, towards the raft, came another Pooper. He was carrying a clump of plastic seaweed from the party display.

"Uh-oh," Holly added. "The Pooper's found them first!"

"Behind you!" yelled Rose.

But the twins were too high up for the Little Sparkles to hear. They watched, horrified, as the Pooper flung the seaweed over the raft, completely covering the Little Sparkles.

"They're trapped," said Holly with a gasp.

"We have to save them," cried Rose. "Quick, let's go down the slide. It's the fastest way to reach them!"

But when Holly looked down the steep, twisting slide, she went white. "It's too high," she gulped.

"Don't worry," said Rose. "We'll go down together."

Holly imagined how frightened the Little Sparkles must be. She took a deep breath.

"They need our help," she said. "I've got to be brave!"

Holly sat in front of Rose, who held her tightly round her middle. Rose pushed off and they zoomed down the

long slide, turning and twisting.

"Are you OK?" asked Rose. But Holly just squealed.

SPLOSH! They shot out of the end of the slide into a shallow pool.

Then Holly laughed. "It was really fun," she said.

They clambered out of the water and

hurried to where the raft was bobbing about in the main pool. The twins could see the Little Sparkles' frightened eyes peeping through the thick seaweed.

"Holly! Rose!" miaowed Tikki. "Save us!"

But the raft had drifted nearer the entrance to the rapids. It began rocking and tilting on the big waves, and then a fast stream of water sucked it into the narrow passageway.

"Help!" cried the Little Sparkles.

"Hold tight," yelled Holly. "We're coming!"

And the twins leapt into the churning water.

4

Something Fishy's Going On

The water in the passageway was rough and fast-flowing, and swept the raft along. The twins let the rapids pull them after it, and paddled as hard as they could to go even faster.

"Nearly there!" gasped Rose.

She gave one last kick and stretched out her arms. Her fingers closed over the edge of the raft.

"You did it!" cried Peppy the puppy.

Holly grabbed the raft too and the girls pulled it back up the rapids. They had to swim against the current, kicking with all their strength. Tubbs bobbed up from under the water and pushed the raft from behind. His little legs moved so quickly that they were a blur.

The twins and Tubbs heaved the raft out of the rapids and into the calm of the main pool. Holly gently pulled the plastic seaweed away from the Little Sparkles. Tinkling delightedly, they floated free, each clutching their party bags. Bubbles the bunny hopped into Holly's arms while Tikki the kitten rubbed against Rose's hand. Princess the pony galloped in a figure-of-eight around the girls.

"You saved us!" barked Peppy. He shook himself, covering the girls in glittering water droplets.

"Of course they did," added Tubbs. "Our twins always make double-trouble for the Poopers!"

There was a snort of laughter from the poolside. It was the Pooper who had thrown the seaweed over the raft.

"Ha, you little weeds, you were nearly sunk!" he sneered. "Try and catch me if you can!"

He ran away down the walkway. Under one of his arms was a bottle of washing-up liquid he must have stolen from Ella's cleaning trolley. The Pooper squirted the slimy liquid over the tiled floor and yelled:

"Slippery-slide,
By the poolside!
Fall over flat,
Your party's gone splat!"

But he was hopping about as he sang, and skidded across the puddle of washing-up liquid. With a frightened shout, he slipped, and had to wave his

arms about to keep upright.

Bubbles held her long ears over her face, as if she couldn't bear to look.

"He's going to hurt himself," Peppy said with a groan.

Holly turned to Rose. "I don't think there's time to try to get him to have fun," she said. "We've got to scare him away before he has an accident."

"I've got an idea!" said Rose.

She leapt out of the pool and went to the pile of inflatable toys heaped by the side. She selected two blow-up sharks that were almost as big as her, though they were as light as balloons. Then she jumped back into the pool and whispered something to Tubbs. He chuckled and ducked under the surface. Rose balanced a toy shark on his back; then she took a deep breath and went underwater. She held on to the underside of the shark so she could move it along the surface.

Holly grinned as she realized what Rose's plan was. The pool was still cloudy from the cola the other Pooper

had tipped into it, so Tubbs and Rose were invisible. It looked like two sharks were swimming through the water!

"Oh no," Holly called to the Pooper. "Sharks!"

The Little Sparkles squealed and pretended to tremble with fright.

"Th-their teeth are all sh-sharp," stammered Peppy.

"They're going to eat us!" wailed Tikki.

Tubbs and Rose moved through the water, so it looked like the sharks were swimming towards the Pooper on the poolside. He backed away, quivering. Then with an ear-piercing yell he dropped the washing-up liquid and scurried away, darting out of the pool exit.

Holly and the Little Sparkles cheered. "Hooray!"

Rose and Tubbs reappeared from the cloudy water.

"Ha! He gave us the slip, didn't he?!" joked Tubbs.

"Phew!" said Rose. "We didn't get to turn him into a Little Sparkle, but at least he's safe. Now where are the other two Poopers?"

5

Catch That Pooper!

"I'm far too brainy to fall for your tricks!" something called from across the pool. "You won't stop me!"

The twins and the Little Sparkles turned in the direction of the voice. One of the Poopers was standing at the other side of the pool, next to a bulging net of blow-up toys. He pulled the net open so that armbands, toys and balls tumbled out and rolled all over the walkway.

Cackling, the Pooper grabbed a blow-up dolphin and yanked out its plug.

HISSSSSSS... The air rushed from the hole.

"Ha! I'm going to flatten all the fun," laughed the Pooper.

"Stop it!" barked Peppy.

"I'll knock you flat too, you little

drip!" The Pooper grabbed a rubber ring and hurled it towards where Peppy and the other Little Sparkles were floating above the pool.

"Look out, everyone!" cried Holly.

The Little Sparkles moved fast. Princess pranced high in the air, Tubbs dived into the water, and Bubbles hopped into Holly's arms. The rubber ring nearly whacked into Peppy and Tikki, but Rose leapt up from the water and caught it in mid-air.

"Cool catch!" said Holly.

"Thanks!" said Rose. She suddenly winked at Holly. "Catch can be a really *fun* game, can't it?"

Holly grinned as she understood what Rose meant. This could be their chance to persuade the Pooper to enjoy himself. If they succeeded, he would turn into a Little Sparkle – and never poop parties again!

"Let's play," Holly called to the Pooper. She threw the rubber ring to him, and he caught it neatly.

"Well done," she said. "Now throw it back!"

"No way," snarled the Pooper. "It's mine now!"

Rose waded through the pool to where the blow-up toys were scattered. She picked up a little duck-shaped toy and lobbed it at the Pooper. He caught it again, but refused to throw the toy back.

"Oh dear," sighed Princess. "I don't think Poopers can play nicely."

Rose looked thoughtfully at a big stripy ball. She picked it up and shouted over to Holly, "Hey, catch!"

Rose threw the ball and Holly spread her arms wide to catch it.

"Now it's your turn," Holly called to the floating Little Sparkles. "Catch!"

She hurled the ball upwards and the Little Sparkles darted through the air to

catch the ball between them. They threw the ball back to Rose, and she passed it to Holly again.

"Not fair," snapped the Pooper. "I want a turn with the ball!"

"But you don't know how to throw

things back," said Holly, tossing the ball to the Little Sparkles.

"I do!" The Pooper stamped his feet. "It's MY turn!"

"OK then, catch!" said Peppy.

The Little Sparkles all gathered beneath the ball. Then they shot upwards, sending it spinning towards the Pooper. He darted towards the ball and seized it with his grubby fingers. "Now I'll show you—"

But his words turned to a screech of surprise. The giant ball didn't stop when he caught it – it carried on bouncing! It bounced away with the Pooper holding on – BOING! BOING! It carried him safely

across the floor and out of the pool door.

The twins and the Little Sparkles laughed. "Our plan didn't work," said Holly, "but at least he can't poop Maisie's—"

She gave a yell as she was covered with water. The final Pooper was coming towards them, hopping across the toys that still floated in the pool. He slapped the water with one of the palm tree leaves. Each time he did so, the twins and the Little Sparkles were covered in spray.

SPLASH! SPLASH!

"It's our last chance today to turn a Pooper into a Little Sparkle," cried Rose. "Stop him!"

6

A Splashy Show-Off

"You won't catch me, you wet blankets," yelled the Pooper, standing on an armband in the middle of the pool. "Splishy-splashy! Your party's trashy!"

The twins swam towards him while the Little Sparkles zoomed above their heads. When they reached the Pooper, he hit the water hard with the palm leaf, soaking Peppy.

The little puppy immediately shook himself. Droplets of water flew from his coat and sprayed over the Pooper.

"Arghhhh!" he shrieked, jumping backwards on to a float. "Don't do that near me, you mucky mutt!"

He bounced away on to a blow-up octopus and then hopped on top of a rubber ring.

"He's escaping!" said Holly. "Split up, and maybe we can stop him."

The twins swam either side of the Pooper. The Little Sparkles skimmed the surface of the water and flew to make a circle around him. As they closed in on the Pooper, he splashed the water harder and harder with his leaf.

SPLASH! SPLASH!

"Oh no," Holly groaned. "Ella's going to think *we're* making the splashes."

As soon as she spoke, there was a shrill whistle. The twins turned towards the sound to see Ella standing by the poolside. She had her mop in one hand

and her whistle in the other.

"No splashing, girls," she called. "Pool rules!"

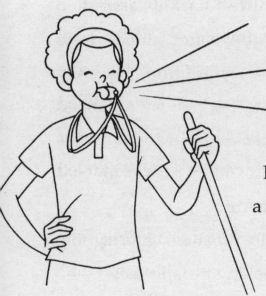

"Sorry!" Rose called. "We won't do it again." Ella gave them a thumbs up and started to walk back to the eating area.

The twins looked back towards the rubber ring where the Pooper was standing – but he was gone.

He had bounced out of the pool and was hurrying along the walkway.

Rose groaned. "He's got us in trouble with Ella, and now he's getting away!"

The twins scrambled out of the pool and followed the Pooper, with the Little Sparkles zooming behind. Holly realized that the Pooper was heading to a corner of the building, towards the steps that led up the big slide.

"He's running into a dead end," she said. "Maybe we can catch him after all."

But the Pooper looked at the long flight of steps, took a deep breath, and bounded up them.

"After him!" cried Rose.

The girls leapt up the steps two at a time with the Sparkles swooping above. Up and up they went, puffing and panting. The Pooper was a few steps ahead of them and looked back over his shoulder.

"Slow-coach children," he crowed.

Soon they were at the top of the steps, beside the entrance to the slide. The Pooper was standing completely still. His grin had faded and he clung to the rail with his hairy knees knocking together.

"It's t-t-too high up here," he said, trembling. "I c-c-can't climb back down all those stairs!"

The twins glanced at each other. "Poor Pooper," whispered Holly. "He's really frightened!"

Rose knelt beside the Pooper. "You won't have to climb down," she said kindly. "You can use the slide instead."

The Pooper stared at the long slide looping to the ground.

"But that looks even more scary than the stairs!" he said, and clung to the railing more tightly.

"No, it's really fun, I promise," said Holly. Then she gave a cry. "Hey, I know!"

Rose and the Little Sparkles gathered around her.

"Let's talk the Pooper into going down the slide," Holly whispered. "Then he might have fun – and turn into a Little Sparkle!"

Rose looked at her watch. "Good plan, but we'll have to hurry. The party starts in five minutes!"

7

It's a Hoot in the chute

"I was scared of the slide at first, too," Holly said to the Pooper. "But then I tried it, and it was brilliant. Have a go!"

But the Pooper shook his head miserably.

"You can do it," Peppy told him.

Tikki stretched her paws out. "Nice hug to wish you luck," she said to the Pooper. She began to sing sweetly.

"Kiss, kiss, cuddle, cuddle,

Hug, hug, snuggle, snuggle..."

The Pooper backed away from the little kitten, making a face like he wanted to be sick.

"Urgh!" he spat. "I'd rather go down the slide than have a disgusting hug."

Holly remembered how sitting in front of Rose had made her feel safe. She crouched at the top of the slide and patted the plastic surface.

"Here," she said to the Pooper, "I'll go down with you. It's less scary if you're with someone else."

Still shaking, the Pooper sat down in

front of Holly. He whimpered and closed his eyes.

"You'll be OK," said Holly, holding him round his lumpy tummy.

"We want to slide down too," Peppy said. Rose sat behind Holly and the tiny Little Sparkles settled in her lap.

"Ready ... steady ... GO!" cried Holly.

WHEEEEE! They were off.

The girls, the Pooper and the Little Sparkles helter-skeltered down the winding slide, whizzing round and round, faster and faster.

"Whoopeeeee!" Rose squealed in delight.

The Pooper made some very odd spluttering sounds. Holly felt his tummy shake beneath her hands.

"Don't worry!" she said. But the Pooper carried on making the strange noises and Holly realized he was chuckling.

"This is so much fun," he giggled.

They all shot out of the end of the slide and landed with a splash in a shallow pool.

Rose and Holly wiped water from their eyes. A glittering mist rose up from the water, and the girls gasped. The Party Pooper had turned into a tiny turquoise seahorse.

"It worked!" cried Rose. "He's a Little Sparkle now!"

"Hip-hip-hooray!" sang Tikki. Princess danced around the seahorse while Tubbs did a roly-poly. Bubbles giggled so much that she got the hiccups.

"Isn't he beautiful," sighed Holly, stroking the little seahorse under the water.

He floated above the surface and giggled. "That tickles!" he said.

Peppy pulled a silver balloon on a ribbon from his party bag. The balloon magically blew itself up and Peppy dangled the string in the water. The seahorse swam up and gripped it with his curly tail.

Together, the Little Sparkles sang:

"Spread the lovely party joy to every
little girl and boy.
No more a grumpy Party Pooper,
make all parties super duper."

Then, holding tightly to his balloon, the tiny seahorse floated gently upwards, out of the water, and through an open window. He was soon a tiny speck against the blue sky. Holly and Rose knew that he wouldn't spoil parties any more – instead, he would do his best to make them fun.

KNOCK KNOCK KNOCK!

The twins looked over to where the sound was coming from. Maisie and the other party guests were outside, waving madly. Billy pressed his face against the glass and made fish faces at them, while Jenny put on her goggles and pretended to swim up and down.

The twins giggled and waved back. Then Rose's face fell.

"The pool's still so messy," she said. "We've got to get it tidy before Maisie sees!"

8

Back in the Swim

"Little Sparkles to the rescue!" yapped Peppy. "We'll fix the muddle with our magic."

He pulled a party blower from his bag and blew it. The Little Sparkles lined up beside him, ready to start tidying the mess made by the Poopers.

"Oh, but wait!" cried Rose. "Ella will see your magic."

"Let's keep her distracted," said Holly.

She took Rose's hand and the twins rushed off to the eating area. Ella was carefully putting the sweets back into the party bags.

"The party's about to start," said Holly. "Can we help you get everything ready?"

Ella nodded gratefully. While they pinned up the plastic seaweed and straightened the anchor, the twins kept Ella talking. Every few moments, they peeped over their shoulders to see what the Little Sparkles were up to.

In a whirl of twinkling colours, the Little Sparkles criss-crossed through the air, sprinkling magical hundreds-and-thousands over the pool. In a moment, the water turned blue and clean again, and the blow-up toys jumped back into their net.

A mop magically appeared on the poolside and washed the tiles until they shone. Tikki scattered silver glitter over the refreshment stand, and in a blink, new bottles of cola appeared on the counter.

When everything was as it should be, Peppy gave a final toot on his trumpet. The Little Sparkles gathered together by the open window.

"It's time to say goodbye to them," Rose whispered to Holly.

Pretending that they were still tidying up, the twins wheeled the cleaning trolley over to the Little Sparkles.

"Thank you for helping us, Holly and Rose," said Peppy.

"We couldn't have done it without you," Tubbs added.

The twins blew kisses to them.

"Goodbye!" called Holly. "See you at the next party!"

Then, in a bright fizzle of colour, the Little Sparkles floated out of the window and disappeared. All that was left was a smudge of glitter in the air.

Ella walked up to the trolley, holding a bottle of cleaning liquid. Suddenly, she stared around the pool, her mouth dropping open in surprise.

"Whoa!" she said. "How did you girls manage to tidy everything so quickly? It's like magic!"

The doors from the changing area swung open. Maisie and the other

boys and girls burst through, wearing their swimming costumes. Maisie's parents were there, too. Her mum was carrying a birthday cake in the shape of a mermaid.

"Happy birthday!" the twins called to Maisie.

"Thanks," Maisie said, giving them each a hug. "I hope you weren't too bored waiting for us."

"Oh no," said Holly, giving her twin a secret glance. "We've had loads of fun already!"

The twins and Maisie went to the edge of the pool. Holly stood in the middle, holding hands with each of them.

"Let's jump in," Holly said. "Ready . . .
steady . . . GO!"

With a happy shout, the three of them jumped into the water together, making a great, big splash.

Don't miss the other
books in the series!

Little Sparkles

Little Sparkles

Party in
the Garden

Have fun with these
tiny magical animals!

Emily Moon

BUBBLES

TIKKI

PEPPY

PRINCESS

TUBBS

Holly and Rose are at the Aqua
Adventure pool. Maisie's having a birthday
party and they've arrived early – just in time for a
quick swim. But all the floats have been thrown
into the water, and the party decorations are spoiled.
Is this the work of the bad Party Poopers?

WHOOOSH!

Out of a locker bursts Tubbs the tiny turtle, and
the other Little Sparkles are close by, too! They're
here to catch those wicked Poopers, and make
the party better than ever.

Cover illustration © Aaron Zenz

6+

ISBN 978-1-407124-58-2

9 781407 124582

■■SCHOLASTIC

£4.99

scholastic.co.uk/zone

'Read on, and discover how to ... sful life'
Sir Richard Branson
from the foreword

Little Wins

THE HUGE POWER
OF THINKING
LIKE A TODDLER

PAUL LINDLEY founder of Ella's kitchen